DO786186

You
Brownie Girl Scout, too!

If you are 6, 7, or 8 years old, or in the 1st, 2nd, or 3rd grade, just ask your parents to look in your local telephone directory under "Girl Scouts," and call for information. You can also ask your parents to call **Girl Scouts of the U.S.A.** at **1-(212) 852-8000** or write to 420 Fifth Avenue, New York, NY 10018-2702 to find out about becoming a Girl Scout in your area.

For all of you who—like Amy
(and me and my daughter)—are the youngest
in your class — M. L.

To my art director, Ronnie Herman
— L.S.L.

Copyright © 1994 by Girl Scouts of the United States of America. All rights reserved. Published by Grosset & Dunlap, Inc., a member of The Putnam & Grosset Group, New York, in cooperation with Girl Scouts of the United States of America. GROSSET & DUNLAP is a trademark of Grosset & Dunlap, Inc. Published simultaneously in Canada. Printed in the U.S.A.

Library of Congress Cataloging-in-Publication Data

Leonard, Marcia.
    Is that really you, Amy? / by Marcia Leonard ; illustrated by
Laurie Struck Long.
        p.   cm. — (Here come the Brownies ; 8)
    Summary: While trying to impress her baby-sitter, who is also a Girl Scout, seven-year-old Amy does not treat her Brownie friends very nicely.
    [1. Girl Scouts—Fiction. 2. Friendship—Fiction. 3. Self-perception—Fiction.]
I. Long, Laurie Struck, ill. II. Title. III. Series.
PZ7.L549Is   1994
[Fic]—dc20   94-19571

ISBN 0-448-40839-2 (pbk.)   B C D E F G H I J
ISBN 0-448-40840-6 (GB)   A B C D E F G H I J

HERE COME THE
BROWNIES
A Brownie Girl Scout Book

Is That Really You, Amy?

By Marcia Leonard
Illustrated by Laurie Struck Long

Grosset & Dunlap • New York
In association with GIRL SCOUTS OF THE U.S.A.

1

"And now, the one, the only, the Amazing Amy on her Flying Trapeze!" Amy called out in her best ringmaster's voice. She was playing circus in her bedroom. Her little sister Andrea was the audience.

Amy had learned how to use a trapeze in gymnastics. And she had a real one hanging from the ceiling of her room.

First she balanced with one leg over the bar. Then she flipped head over heels. Turning once. Turning twice.

Andrea clapped and bounced up and down on Amy's bed. "Me do it! Me do it!" she cried.

Amy hung by her knees. "No, Andrea. You can't. You'll have to wait until you are *much* older. Like me."

Andrea's face grew stormy. Her chubby hands curled into fists.

Uh-oh, thought Amy. She flipped down from the trapeze. Lately, Andrea had temper tantrums all the time. Amy's parents said it was the terrible twos.

Andrea opened her mouth to shriek—and the doorbell rang.

Whew! thought Amy. Saved by the bell.

"That's Hallie!" she told her sister quickly. "Mom said she was coming over."

Instantly Andrea was all smiles again. Hallie was her favorite baby-sitter. She took

Amy's hand and tugged her toward the stairs.

Hallie was thirteen. And she was Amy's favorite sitter, too. For one thing, she treated Amy more like a friend than a little kid. For another, they were both Girl Scouts. Amy was a Brownie. And Hallie was a Cadette.

Downstairs, Amy's mom was hanging up Hallie's black jacket. All of Hallie's clothes were black or white. Only her jewelry was colorful. Tonight she had on a choker with a bright blue pendant.

"Hi, guys!" Hallie tossed back her silky, straight black hair. She knelt down, and Andrea ran to give her a hug.

"So," Hallie winked at Amy. "How has Ms. Andrea been today?"

It was a game they played whenever Hallie came over. Amy pretended she was a baby-sitter, too. And they took care of Andrea together.

Amy rolled her eyes. "Well, you know the terrible twos. She had a good dinner. But she threw her lima beans on the floor."

"Yucky yima beans," said Andrea.

"They're good for you," said Amy.

"We'll be at the movies. The number is by the phone," Amy's mom told Hallie. "You can put Andrea to bed after her bath. But Amy can stay up till 8:30 as a special treat."

Amy punched the air with her fist. "All right! Thanks, Ma."

After Amy's parents left, Hallie tiptoed

up behind Andrea. "Okay, Andrea. Bathtime!" she said.

"No bath," squealed Andrea. She ran away, giggling like crazy.

This was part of their game, too.

"I'm going to get you," called Hallie. She chased Andrea. Caught her. And carried her up to the bathroom. Then she got Andrea undressed while Amy ran the water.

"Not too hot and not too cold," said Amy.

"Just right!" said Hallie. She lifted Andrea into the tub.

When bathtime was over, Amy read Andrea a story. Then Hallie tucked her into bed. And they both sang Andrea's favorite song: "Skinamarink-a-dinky-dink, Skinamarink-a-doo, I Love You."

The third time through, Hallie gave Amy

the thumbs-up sign. Andrea was fast asleep. They tiptoed out of the room and back downstairs.

"What a team," Hallie said as they flopped onto the sofa.

"Yeah, we're the dream team!" Amy grinned. Hallie's words made her feel good.

Hallie glanced at her watch. "So, what do you want to do now?"

Amy thought hard. She didn't want to choose anything too babyish. But she wasn't sure what eighth-graders did for fun.

"Um—you choose," she said at last.

"Well, there's a hairstyle I've been dying to try," said Hallie. "My hair is too straight. But yours would be perfect. Want to be my model?"

"Sure!" said Amy. She ran and got her brush and comb, and some barrettes and

clips. She undid her braid. Then she sat on the floor in front of Hallie.

Hallie started brushing. "You'll never guess where I saw this style."

Amy thought a moment. "In a magazine?"

"Nope. On a doll."

"What?" Amy jerked her head around.

"Hey! Hold still," said Hallie. "Trust me. You're going to look great."

"With a *doll* hairdo?" squeaked Amy.

"Not any old doll. A gorgeous antique doll I saw at the new Elizabeth Jordan Toy Museum." Hallie divided Amy's hair into sections. "My Cadette troop has been helping out since the museum opened. Now we give tours!"

"Hey, maybe we could take your tour! I mean, me and my whole Brownie troop. I could bring it up at our next meeting."

"That'd be fun!" said Hallie.

She fastened a last clip in Amy's hair.
Then she leaned back to see the effect.
"Wow! Is that really *you*, Amy? You look
so much older. Come and see for yourself."
She led Amy over to the front hall mirror.

Amy stared at her reflection. Soft wisps
of hair framed her face. The rest was French
braided and drawn up on top of her head.
She looked very elegant. And very grown-
up. Like a princess . . . or a movie star.

"Cool," she said.

"Way cool," said Hallie.

2

When Amy went to bed, she left her hair pinned up. She couldn't wait to show her friends at school her new style.

She imagined walking into Mrs. Fujikawa's class the next day. All the kids would notice how grown-up she looked. She might be the youngest kid in 2-B. But she was way cool.

But when Amy woke up, her hair was a mess. She tried to fix it the way Hallie had.

But she ended up looking more like a clown than a movie star.

Sighing, she brushed out the tangles and braided her hair as usual. Then to cheer herself up, she tied two ribbons—a blue one and a brown one—around the end of her braid. Blue and brown were Brownie Girl Scout colors. And her troop was meeting that afternoon.

After school, Amy, her best friend Corrie, and the other Brownies from her class headed for the lunchroom. That's where their troop met every Friday.

Amy couldn't wait to share her idea about the museum tour. But the minute she saw her troop leader, Mrs. Quinones, she forgot all about it.

Mrs. Q. was up on a stepladder. In her arms was the biggest piñata Amy had ever seen. It was a snowy white unicorn with a flowing pink mane and tail. Its horn and hooves were silver.

"*¡Que lindo!*" breathed Corrie. That meant "how beautiful" in Spanish. Amy knew because Corrie had been teaching her how to say a few words.

Mrs. Q. hung the piñata from a hook in the ceiling. Carefully, she let out the string. The unicorn pranced in midair.

"Wow!" said Lauren. "Where did that come from, Mrs. Q.?"

"Sarah," Mrs. Q. said, "would you like to explain while we have our snack?"

Sarah cleared her throat. She was shy about speaking in front of people—even her own Brownie troop.

"Um—my grandma got the piñata in Mexico. It has little toys and candy inside. A piñata is supposed to be for your birthday. But I won't be eight for another two months, and I just couldn't wait."

Eight! Amy thought with surprise. Sarah is nearly eight! And I'm just barely seven. I really hate being the class baby.

"So here's the good news," Mrs. Q. went on. "Sarah's decided to share her piñata with us now!" She held up a blindfold and a long wooden broomstick. "Sarah? Want to go first?"

Sarah shrugged, but stepped forward.

Mrs. Q. blindfolded her and handed her the stick. Then Marsha and Lauren turned her around and around.

"You have three tries to break the piñata," said Lauren. "Go for it, Sarah!"

Sarah swung—and missed by a mile. Her next two swings were as wild as her first.

"Someone else can try now." Sarah sounded relieved.

One by one, the girls took their best shots.

Krissy A. hit the piñata on her third swing. But not hard enough to break it.

Krissy S. got dizzy from the spinning and walked into a wall.

Lauren smacked a table, the flagpole, and then the unicorn. But it still didn't break.

Amy was getting impatient for her turn. She knew she would break the piñata—on the first try!

But Jo Ann was up next. As she missed her third swing, Amy yelled, "Striiiiike three! You're out!" like a baseball umpire.

Jo Ann laughed. "Okay—you try it," she said. "It's harder than you think."

Amy put on the blindfold. "Just watch the pro," she said. She held the stick the way a baseball player holds a bat.

"Wait a minute," said Marsha. She and Lauren spun Amy around.

Suddenly Amy knew why no one had broken the piñata yet. She didn't have a clue where it was! She swung and missed. Once. Twice. Three times.

"Strike three! *You're* out," said Jo Ann.

Amy pulled off the blindfold. She shot Jo Ann a dirty look. "Very funny," she said.

Jo Ann held up both hands. "Hey, Amy. Don't dish it out, if you can't take it."

Amy turned away. She was mad. But at herself. First because she'd struck out. She was usually good at games. And second because Jo Ann was right. She hadn't been a good sport. It was something Mrs. Fujikawa said she needed "to work on." After all, only babies were poor sports.

It was Sharnelle's turn next. She swung hard. CRACK! The piñata split open. And out fell a shower of goodies.

Instantly, Amy forgot her bad mood. She dove for the treasure on the floor along with

the other girls. When she stood
up she had a
tiny sparkly pencil, two
cherry lollipops, and
a necklace of hot pink beads.
She liked the necklace best.
It reminded her of Hallie.

She went over to Corrie.
"Check out this loot," she said.
"What did you get?"

Corrie rolled her eyes. "Not
much!" She held up a plastic baby
rattle and a bright green lollipop.
"Lime. My un-favorite."

Amy handed Corrie a cherry lollipop.
"Here—have one of mine. Take the tiny
pencil, too—you can draw tiny pictures!"

"Thanks, Amy!" Corrie admired the
pencil. "What a good idea."

Amy grinned. "Hey—if you like that idea, wait till you hear my next one!" Amy waved at Mrs. Q. "There's something I want to talk about," Amy told her. "Could we make a Brownie ring?"

"Of course," said Mrs. Q. She gathered the girls together in a circle. Then Amy told them about Hallie and the Cadette Girl Scouts and the toy museum.

"I really want to take the Cadettes' tour," Amy finished. "And I thought you guys might like to go, too."

"Shall we take a vote?" asked Mrs. Q. "All those in favor of the tour—"

At once, every girl raised her hand.

"That makes it unanimous, Amy," Mrs. Q. said. "I'll call Mrs. Webster, the Cadettes' troop leader, and set it up."

3

A week later, the Brownies were standing in the grand hall of the Elizabeth Jordan Toy Museum. They stared at the high carved ceiling and the fancy curved staircase.

"Can you believe this was once somebody's home?" said Amy. "It's humongous!"

"Think of climbing all the stairs," said Corrie.

"Think of sliding down all the banisters!" said Amy.

Amy spied Hallie across the room. She had on a floaty black dress, a long white scarf, and black high-top sneakers. She was standing with three other Cadettes.

Amy waved. And Hallie waved back.

Mrs. Webster welcomed the Brownie Girl Scouts, and a Cadette named Erin told them a little bit about the museum. Then Hallie asked them to divide up into groups of five for the tour. "Each group will have two Cadette guides," she explained.

Amy was in a group with Corrie, Sarah, Krissy S., and Sharnelle. Hallie and another Cadette joined them.

"Janet and I will take you guys," Hallie said. She gave Amy's shoulder a squeeze. "This tour was Amy's idea. And she and I are kind of a team already."

Janet smiled at Amy. "Let's start in the

parlor," she said to the group.

She and Hallie led the girls into a long, fancy room with a big marble fireplace. There was no furniture. Instead the room was full of antique dollhouses in big glass cases.

"Ooooh!" breathed the girls. They wandered from case to case, pointing and staring at all the little rooms and tiny furniture.

Hallie showed them her favorite. "It's a

miniature version of this very house," she said. "You can see how it looked long ago, when Elizabeth Jordan and her family lived in it."

"It looks so real, I almost expect to see *me* in it—right here, by the fireplace," said Amy. She posed by the mantel.

"Welcome to my humble home," she said in a fake English accent. "The butler will bring tea."

The other girls laughed.

Hallie bowed like a butler. "If Madam allows, we will tour the music room first."

"Certainly," Amy said in her fancy voice.

The music room was full of mechanical toys. Amy's favorite was a circus with an acrobat on a flying trapeze.

Next Hallie led them upstairs to a large, sunny room.

"Wow, look at all the dolls!" said Amy.

There were dolls made of wood and dolls made of wax. Bride dolls and ballerina dolls. Baby dolls and rag dolls.

Amy nudged Hallie. "Okay. So where's the one with *my* hairdo?"

Hallie pointed to a case. Inside was a doll with a delicate china face and blond braids drawn up on top of her head. She was posed as if she were packing for a trip. Dresses and petticoats were draped over her bed. And an old-fashioned wooden trunk stood open beside her.

"Cool!" said Amy.

"Way cool," said Hallie.

"I wonder where she's going," said Amy.

"Paris, France," Hallie said at once. She tossed back her hair. "That's where I'm going when I finish college."

"Me, too," said Amy. If Hallie wanted to go to Paris, then she did, too.

The next room was full of antique stuffed animals. One wall held nothing but teddy bears. There was also a life-size zebra, and a wooden Noah's ark with all the animals lined up two by two.

Then Janet and Hallie led the way to the third floor. Up here were toy cars, trucks, fire engines—and all kinds of old model boats and planes.

"And we've saved the best for last," Hallie said, flinging open a door.

There in the middle of the room was an enormous train set. It was laid out on a raised platform, so people could walk around it.

Hallie flipped a switch. Like magic, lights went on all over the set and the train started up. It chugged along the track—over mountains, through tunnels, and past little towns. Through the lit window of a train station, Amy saw tiny people sitting reading tiny newspapers.

"That was a great tour!" Amy told Hallie as they headed back downstairs.

"I'm glad you liked it," Hallie said. "It wouldn't have happened without you!"

Amy smiled. Then she sneaked a peek at the other girls to make sure they were listening.

Amy's group met the other Brownies in the dining room. Corrie stopped by one of the tables. "Let's sit here," she said, pulling out a chair for Amy.

But Amy didn't sit down. "Um—I want to ask Hallie something. I'll be right back."

Corrie shrugged. "Okay, I'll save you a seat."

The Cadettes were getting ready to serve the snack—punch, strawberries, and little sandwiches cut in triangle pieces.

Amy made her way over to Hallie.

"Need any help?" she asked.

Hallie handed her a stack of paper napkins. "Thanks—you're a lifesaver! Pass these out, would you?"

"Sure!" said Amy.

She put a napkin at each place. Then Janet gave her cups of punch to pass out. And before she knew it, Amy had helped serve the entire snack!

"Come sit with me and Janet, Amy," Hallie said when they were through. "I want you to meet some of my other friends."

Amy didn't need to be asked twice. She was thrilled to sit with the older girls.

"Meet Erin and Maya," said Hallie.

The Cadettes joked with Amy. And they asked her all about Brownie Girl Scouts—

what Try-It patches she had earned, and when she would fly up to Juniors.

From the corner of her eye, Amy saw the empty chair next to Corrie. Ooops! She really should have told Corrie she was sitting with Hallie. But Corrie looked as if she were having fun. And Amy knew she would understand.

Right now, Amy liked all the attention the Cadettes were giving her. She liked making them laugh. And most of all, she liked the grown-up way she felt around the older girls. It made her feel special and cool. Way cool!

4

Over the weekend, Amy sorted through her clothes. Anything babyish, she tossed aside. That didn't leave her much to wear. But it was better than dressing like a little kid.

Amy also started wearing her hair down—like Hallie. Sometimes it got tangled. And sometimes she missed her braid. But she was sure she looked much more grown-up.

At school on Monday, Corrie noticed her new look right away.

"I like your hair!" she told Amy.

"Thanks!" Amy flipped her hair back the way Hallie did. "Um—by the way," she said. "Sorry I didn't sit with you at the museum. Hallie wanted me to meet some of her friends."

"That's okay." Corrie smiled at Amy. "Boy, that place is great! I'd like to go back sometime. Maybe Hallie could give us a private tour."

"I'm sure I could arrange it," Amy said importantly. She gave her hair another flip.

But as it turned out, Amy didn't have to arrange a thing.

"Look what came in the mail!" Mrs. Q. said at the troop meeting on Friday. She held up a piece of paper. "See if you can figure out what this is."

The girls crowded around her.

"It's a rebus!" Krissy A. said quickly.

"What kind of bus?" asked a first grader named Lucy.

"Not a *bus*. A *rebus*. A kind of puzzle with pictures instead of words," replied Krissy A. "Look at the first line."

There was a little drawing of a deer. Then a patch of brown. Then a pair of legs, with an arrow pointing at the knees.

"The message is, 'deer brown knees,'" Krissy explained.

"Oh! I get it!" cried Amy. "'Dear Brownies.' It's a letter to us!"

"Let's figure out the rest," said Lauren.

The girls studied the page. Soon they had decoded the message.

"Dear Brownies," it said. "You are invited to a treasure hunt and tea party at the toy museum, 4:30 Sunday."

"It's from 'Mrs. Web Star.' That's Mrs. Webster, Hallie's troop leader," said Amy.

"So what do you want to tell 'Mrs. Web Star'?" Mrs. Q. asked.

"Yes!" they all shouted. "We want to go!"

The girls spent the rest of the meeting writing thank-you notes to the Cadettes. Amy and Corrie did theirs together. Amy wrote the words. And Corrie drew tiny pictures of trains and dolls and teddy bears with her tiny pencil.

"Very nice, girls," Mrs. Q. said when they finished. "You make good partners."

"Thanks, Mrs. Q.," said Corrie. She turned to Amy. "Maybe we can be partners for the Cadettes' treasure hunt, too."

"Sure," said Amy. "That is—if Hallie doesn't need me to help."

Corrie gave her a funny look. But Amy didn't notice. She was already planning what she'd wear on Sunday.

5

"Hurry up, honey, or you'll be late for the treasure hunt," Amy's mother called. "Your ride will be here any minute."

"Coming, Ma!" Amy took one last look in the mirror. She was wearing black leggings, white sneakers, and a long, white cotton top. The top was really a beach cover-up. But she didn't think anyone would notice. Besides, it looked great with the hot pink beads she'd gotten from the piñata.

"My! You look...different," said her

mom as Amy hurried down the stairs.

Suddenly, Amy was worried about her clothes. "Different, yucky? Or different, nice?" she asked.

"Different nice," said her mom. "But the outfit looks more like Hallie than you."

Amy grinned. That was the idea.

The doorbell rang.

"That's my ride. See you, Ma." Amy kissed her mother and hurried out the door.

As soon as Amy got to the museum, she ran into Janet.

"Hey, cute outfit. New hairstyle?" Janet asked.

Amy nodded, glad that Janet had noticed. She tossed back her hair. "It's more me— don't you think?"

Janet smiled then pointed across the room. "Hallie's over there, if you're looking for her."

Hallie was busy reading some colored index cards.

"Hi," said Amy. "I was just wondering— do you need any help today?"

Hallie looked up. "Oh, hi, Amy," she said. "Thanks for offering. But I think you should enjoy the treasure hunt. I kind of had you in mind when we planned it."

"Oh—I hope my team wins," said Amy.

She really wanted Hallie to be proud of her.

Before the treasure hunt began, Hallie's friend Maya had the Brownies divide into teams. Amy was with Corrie, Sarah, Marsha, and Jo Ann.

"Each team will have a color," Maya explained. "And you'll follow a trail of clues written on that color card. They will lead you to the treasure."

Then Hallie handed out the cards. Amy's team got blue—her favorite color. Marsha read the clue out loud.

"Riddle: Why doesn't an elephant have to pack a suitcase? Answer: Because he always carries his trunk! To find your next clue, find another kind of trunk."

"Maybe it's a tree trunk," said Jo Ann.

"There were trees all over the train set," said Corrie.

"No, no! It's not *that* kind of trunk,"
Amy said quickly. "Follow me! I know
where the next clue is."

Amy rushed off. She led the other girls
upstairs to the doll room, right to the blond
doll with the wooden trunk. Another blue
card was taped to the glass case.

"I knew it! Here's the clue!" Amy
crowed.

Sarah read it. "In came the animals, two
by two. This boat is a floating zoo. Find it
and you'll have your next clue."

"I know—it's the Noah's ark. It's in the
stuffed animal room!" said Corrie.

Amy was already heading out the door.
"Come on. Let's go!" she called.

Sure enough, stuck to the Noah's ark
case was another blue card. Amy snatched
it up.

You can ride on a bike,
in a taxi or bus.
You can ride in a car
to come visit us.
And there's something else
you can ride in, it's true.
Just guess what it is
to find the next clue.

"Something else you ride in," Marsha repeated.

"It's the train," said Amy. "Come on!"

"Wait a second," said Jo Ann. "It could also be a plane or a boat."

"Yeah! A model plane! That's probably it," agreed Corrie.

"You might be right. Maybe we should take a vote," said Marsha.

They did, and airplanes won. Four to one.

"You're all wrong. You'll see. I bet it's the train," Amy said.

"Well, we'll never know if we just stand here," said Jo Ann. "Last one up the stairs is a rotten egg!"

As the girls headed for the third floor, the yellow team came down the stairs.

"How's it going?" Marsha called to Lauren.

"Great!" Lauren called back. "We're on clue number four."

Amy's heart sank. Her team was only on clue number three! At this rate, they would finish last. What would Hallie think of her then?

They searched the third-floor rooms for their next clue. But it was not with the model planes—or even the boats.

"I told you! It's the train!" Amy was

practically shouting. "Let's go. We're way behind."

Amy dashed off to the train room. The other girls followed a little more slowly.

Just as Amy had thought, there was a blue card taped to the train platform. "See!" she said, handing the card to Corrie.

"Okay, okay," said Corrie. Then she read the message. "To find the next clue, unscramble these letters: T-R-A-B-O-C-A."

There was a pad of paper and some pencils by the train set. The girls got to work.

"BRACTOA. ACTOBAR. RATACOB," said Amy.

"How about ABRACOT?" said Sarah. "That sounds like a fruit."

Marsha giggled. "Or maybe

CRABOAT—a special boat for catching crabs. Or ROBACAT—to steal from cats."

Now the other girls were laughing, too. All except Amy.

"Come on, you guys. You've wasted enough time already!" she fumed. "You're acting like silly babies."

"And you're acting like a big pain!" said Marsha. "We're just having fun."

"Besides, who are you calling a baby?" teased Jo Ann. "You're the youngest in the class. Remember?"

Amy's face burned. She wished she could leave. But she didn't want to let Hallie down. So she just stared at her paper, trying to make the letters form a real word.

Suddenly, Sarah looked up. "I've got it," she said quietly. "The answer is ACROBAT."

"The mechanical circus!" cried Marsha.

The girls headed downstairs. On the way, they passed another team. The girls all looked pretty confused. Amy gave a mental cheer. Maybe her team could still win!

The acrobat's clue sent the girls on to the parlor—to the museum dollhouse. In the dollhouse ballroom was a circle of Brownie pins.

"That's supposed to be us!" shouted Amy. "The treasure is in the ballroom! Let's run for it."

The girls burst through the doors—with Amy in the lead.

The ballroom was all decorated for a tea party. Tables were set up—and each one had a bouquet of balloons tied to a china teapot. There was even a bag of chocolate coins at each place.

Amy scanned the room. Had her team won? Her shoulders slumped. No. They hadn't. Lauren's team was already sitting down.

"I can't believe it," she said. "We came in second."

Jo Ann, Marsha, and Sarah didn't seem upset by the news. They were busy opening their bags of treasure candy.

"Hey, don't feel bad," said Corrie. "Let's find our seats."

But Amy turned away. "I want to find Hallie and Janet," was all she said.

Corrie's face fell as Amy stomped off.

Hallie was nowhere in sight. But Amy soon spied Janet and Maya. They were putting cookies on a platter. Their backs were toward her.

Amy was just about to say hi, when she heard her own name.

"That Amy is my favorite Brownie," Maya was saying.

"Mine, too. She's so funny!" added Janet.

Amy's spirits lifted like a helium balloon. They were talking about her!

Janet went on. "Did you notice that she's copying the way Hallie dresses? And the way Hallie tosses back her hair? That little kid is so cute, I can hardly stand it."

Now Amy's stomach did flip-flops. She felt cold and faint. They thought she was just a cute little kid. A cute little *copycat* kid! They didn't think she was one of them at all.

The yucky feeling in her stomach started climbing to her throat. And what about

Hallie? Hallie probably thought she was the dumbest kid ever!

Amy backed off quickly. What if Maya and Janet spotted her! Or worse yet, Hallie?

She started toward the tables. Then she froze. There was no way she could face her teammates either—especially not Corrie.

Looking back, she wasn't proud of the way she'd acted. She'd been rude to Corrie. And she'd been a poor sport. Really, *she'd* been the baby, not her friends.

Amy felt like a mouse with no hole to hide in. What could she do? Where could she go? When would this terrible party be over?

6

"Amy? Are you all right?" Mrs. Q. bent down to look into Amy's eyes. "Is something wrong?"

Amy nodded miserably. "Ev-everything," she mumbled.

"Do you want to tell me about it?" Mrs. Q. asked gently. "Let's go over where it's quiet." She led Amy into the hallway.

Amy took a deep breath. "I've been acting really dumb," she said at last. She told Mrs. Q. about copying Hallie. And trying to act like a big kid. And getting mad at her teammates. And then she told her what Janet and Maya had said.

"Let's talk about the Cadettes first," suggested Mrs. Q. "It sounds to me as if they said a lot of good things about you."

"Well—they did say I was funny," Amy said slowly. "And they said that I was their favorite Brownie."

"Those are very good things," said Mrs. Q.

Amy started to smile. Then she frowned. "But Janet said it was *cute* the way I was copying Hallie. And I don't want to be cute. Or a copycat."

"Then just be yourself, Amy," said Mrs. Q. "That's the girl the Cadettes really like. And the Brownies, too."

"I guess you're right," Amy said.

"Thanks, Mrs. Q. I feel a lot better."

"I'm glad," said Mrs. Q. "There's a whole lot of party left to enjoy!"

Amy nodded. "But first there's something I need to tell my friends."

Slowly, she made her way back into the ballroom. And right away, Corrie waved her over.

"Amy! We saved you a seat."

"Thanks...but first, there's something I want to say." Amy looked around the table. "I'm really sorry about the way I acted on the treasure hunt. I like winning. And sometimes I forget that games are for fun."

"We know." Corrie smiled. "But we like you anyway."

"Apology accepted," said Jo Ann. She held up a plate of cookies. "Now that you're back, could you help us finish these?"

Amy felt a wave of relief. Suddenly she was starving. "Nothing comes between me and a chocolate chip cookie!" she said.

At least her friends weren't mad at her. But Hallie! How could she ever face Hallie again?

When it was time for the Brownies to say good-bye, Amy tried to be invisible. But Hallie caught up with her as she was going out the door.

"Bye, Amy," Hallie called. "See you soon!"

"Bye," mumbled Amy. Then she ducked her head and hurried outside.

Amy hoped she wouldn't see Hallie for a long, long time. Long enough for Hallie to forget how she'd tried to act like a big kid. How she'd been a silly copycat.

A year or two ought to do it, she figured.

7

The next morning, Amy braided her hair. Then she quickly sorted through her clothes again. Some outfits really were too babyish. She set those aside for Andrea to grow into. She put the rest back into her closet. And she tossed the hot pink beads into her dress-up box.

For the next few days she tried not to think about Hallie. But it wasn't easy.

Then after dinner on Thursday, Amy's mom said, "There's frozen yogurt for dessert. Do you girls want it now? Or later, when Hallie's here?"

"Now, Mommy," said Andrea.

"Hallie's coming here?" squeaked Amy.

"Why so surprised?" asked her dad. "Hallie always baby-sits when we go to the movies."

Amy did not want to see Hallie. "Um— could I go over to Corrie's?" she asked.

"No, honey. It's a school night," her mom reminded her.

"Oh, right." Amy got up quickly. "Well, I think I'll go upstairs now. I have a lot of reading to do."

She hurried to her room and closed the door. Then she stacked a big pile of books on her desk and opened the first one. Her plan was to look as busy as possible when Hallie arrived.

Soon Amy heard the doorbell ring. But she didn't move. A few minutes later, Hallie tapped on her door.

"Come in," Amy said nervously.

Hallie was wearing a short, fuzzy white sweater, black jeans, and a necklace of red hearts. She had Andrea by the hand.

"Hi," she said. "I was wondering where my partner was. Want to help give Ms. Andrea her bath?"

"Oh, I can't," said Amy. "I've got all this reading to do." She pointed to the books.

"That's okay." Hallie nodded. "Next time." And she closed the door.

Amy breathed a sigh of relief. Now she would just stay in her room till bedtime.

She started to read again. But she never got past page one. She found herself listening instead. First to the sound of running water. Then to Hallie getting Andrea ready for bed. Then to Andrea crying and yelling.

Andrea was having a major temper tantrum!

Minutes passed. Amy could hear Hallie

trying to calm Andrea down. But the yelling just got louder.

At last, Amy got up from her desk. It didn't matter how embarrassed she felt. She had to try to help. She hurried to Andrea's room.

"Amy! Am I glad to see you," said Hallie. "Andrea won't go to bed. Maybe you can do something." Hallie looked desperate.

"I'll try," said Amy. She knelt down and gently held her sister until she was calm.

"What's wrong, Andrea?" she asked. "Can you tell me what you want?"

"Want—want—Hallie *and* you," Andrea said between sobs.

Hallie tossed back her hair. "Of course! Andrea's used to having both of us put her to bed. The dream team, remember?"

"I remember," said Amy. "Come on, Andrea. I'll read you a story. And Hallie will tuck you in. Then we'll both sing you a song. Okay?"

Andrea nodded, rubbing her eyes.

This time, Amy and Hallie only had to sing "Skinamarink-a-dinky-dink" once. Then they tiptoed into the hall.

"Whew!" said Hallie. "Thanks for the help, partner!" She grinned at Amy. "Hey, your mom said we could have some frozen yogurt. Want some? Or do you have to get back to your reading?"

Reading? Amy had forgotten all about it. To her surprise, she felt comfortable with Hallie.

"Oh, I'm done for tonight," she said.

"Good," said Hallie. "I think we deserve an extra scoop of frozen yogurt."

"*And* some chocolate sauce," said Amy.

"I've been meaning to ask you," Hallie said when they were settled in the kitchen. "Did you have a good time at the treasure hunt? You seemed kind of quiet at the end."

"Well, I wasn't feeling so great," Amy said honestly. Then suddenly it hit her. Hallie was treating her the way she always

had. As a partner and a special friend.
Maybe Hallie hadn't even noticed the
copycatting. And even if she had, it didn't
seem to matter.

"I'm sorry you felt bad," Hallie told her.
"You're all better now?"

"Yep!" Amy smiled. "I'm back to my
old self again!"